HOW TO DRAW CATS

Barbara Soloff Levy

DOVER PUBLICATIONS, INC.
Mineola, New York

Note

Drawing a picture of your favorite kitty may seem scary, but it's easy! By following the simple diagrams in this book, not only can you draw your pet sleeping, stretching, sitting, standing and playing, you can also draw lions, tigers, cheetahs and other wild cats as well. To show you how easy it is, let's draw the sitting cat on page 1. You will be doing some erasing, so use a pencil, not a pen. First, draw a large circle for the body with an oval on top of it for the head. Next, add the ears, tail and front legs; erase the part of the body that cuts through the legs, as indicated by the broken lines. Now, add the back legs. Finally, add the eyes, nose, mouth, whiskers, inner ears and toes. What could be simpler!

Copyright

Copyright © 1997 by Barbara Soloff Levy.
All rights reserved under Pan American and International Copyright Conventions.

Published in Canada by General Publishing Company, Ltd., 30 Lesmill Road, Don Mills, Toronto, Ontario.

Bibliographical Note

How to Draw Cats is a new work, first published by Dover Publications, Inc., in 1997.

Library of Congress Cataloging-in-Publication Data

Soloff-Levy, Barbara.
    How to draw cats / Barbara Soloff Levy.
        p.   cm.
    ISBN 0-486-29621-0 (pbk.)
    1. Cats in art.   2. Drawing—Technique.   I. Title.
NC783.8.C36S66 1997
743.6'975—dc21   96-47816
                                                                        CIP

Manufactured in the United States of America
Dover Publications, Inc., 31 East 2nd Street, Mineola, N.Y. 11501

1

2

6   Manx

8

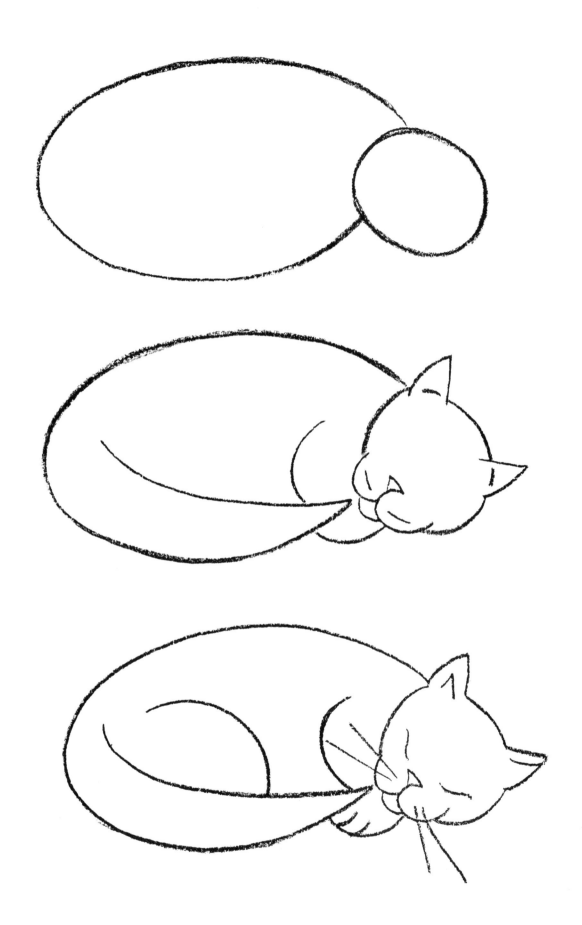

13

Tiger   25

Leopard 27

28   Lioness

Lion 29

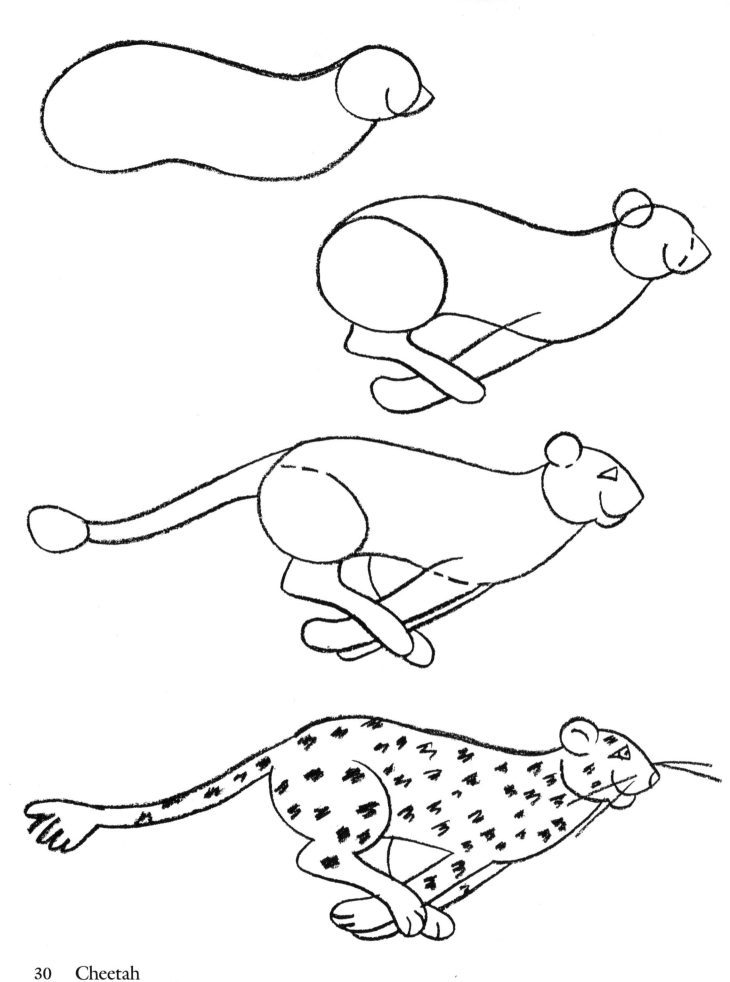

30   Cheetah